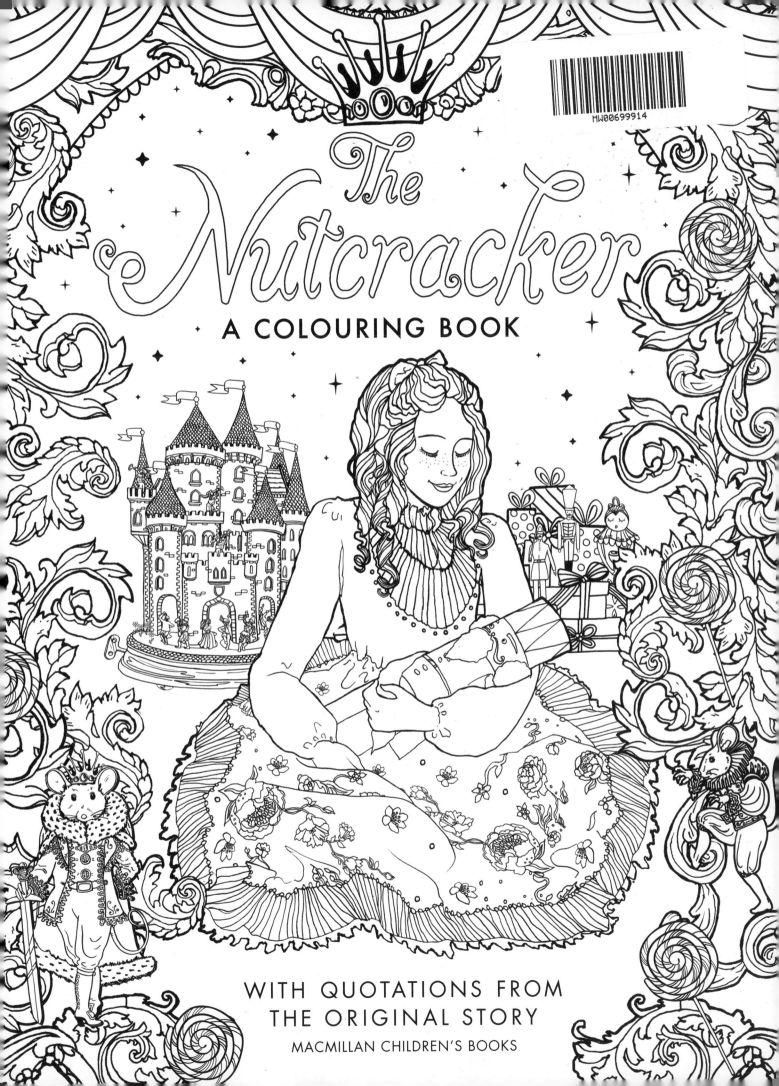

The Nutcracker

A COLOURING BOOK

WITH QUOTATIONS FROM
THE ORIGINAL STORY

MACMILLAN CHILDREN'S BOOKS

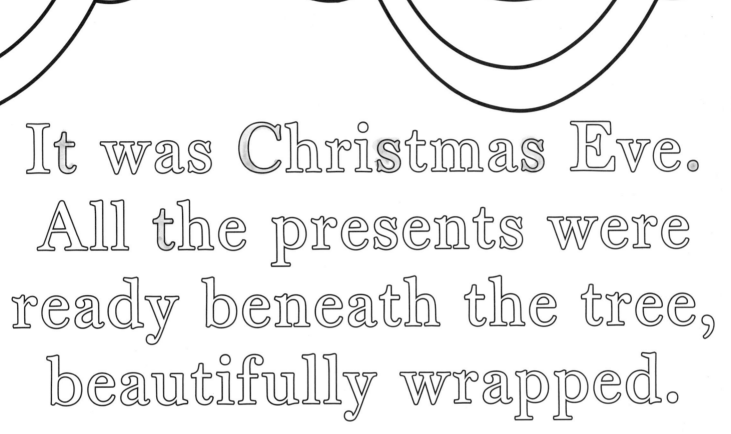

It was Christmas Eve.
All the presents were
ready beneath the tree,
beautifully wrapped.

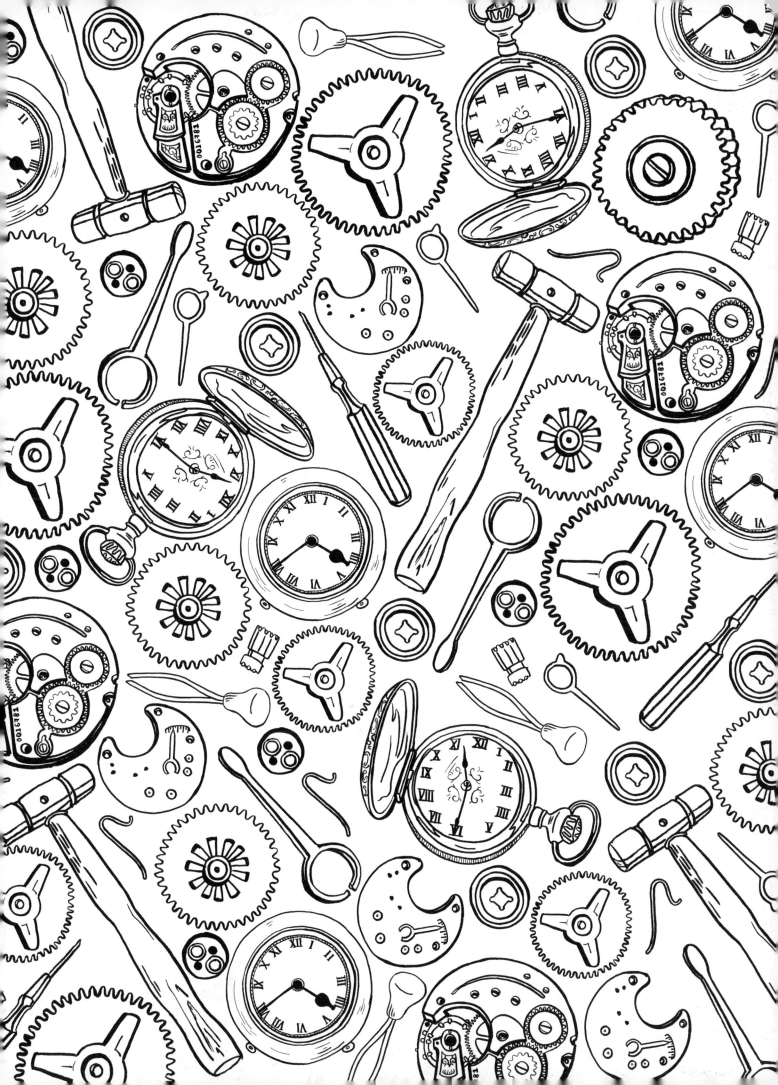

Godfather Drosselmeyer
was making a beautiful
present for the children.

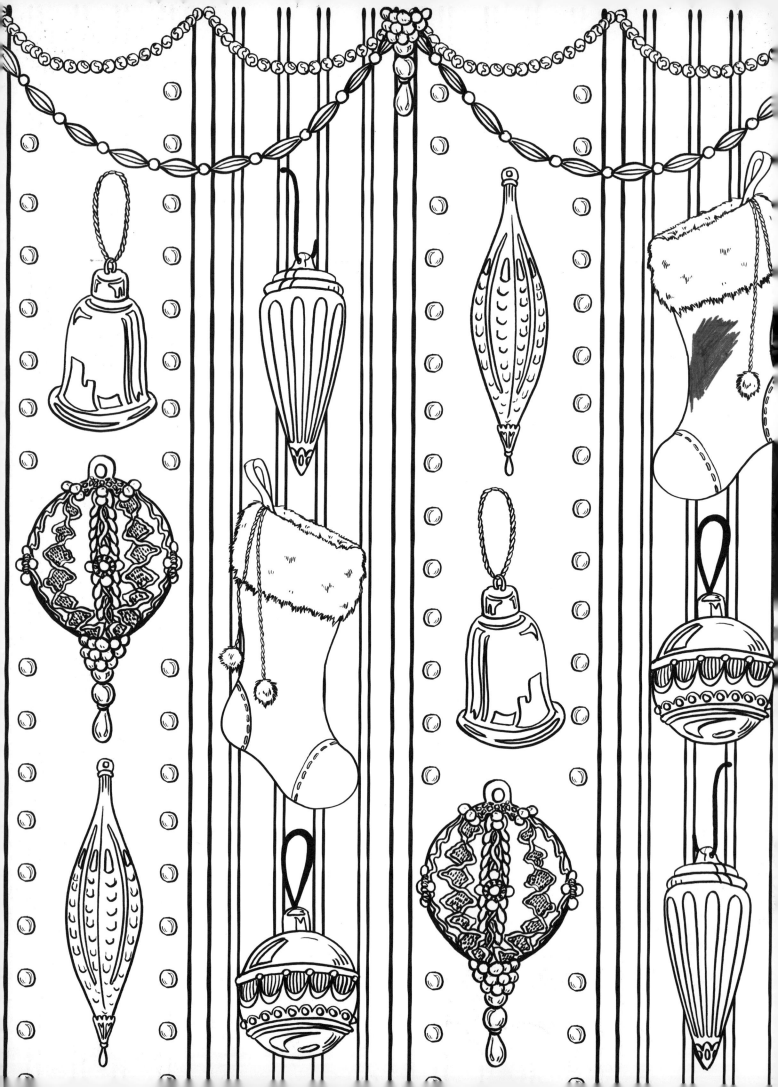

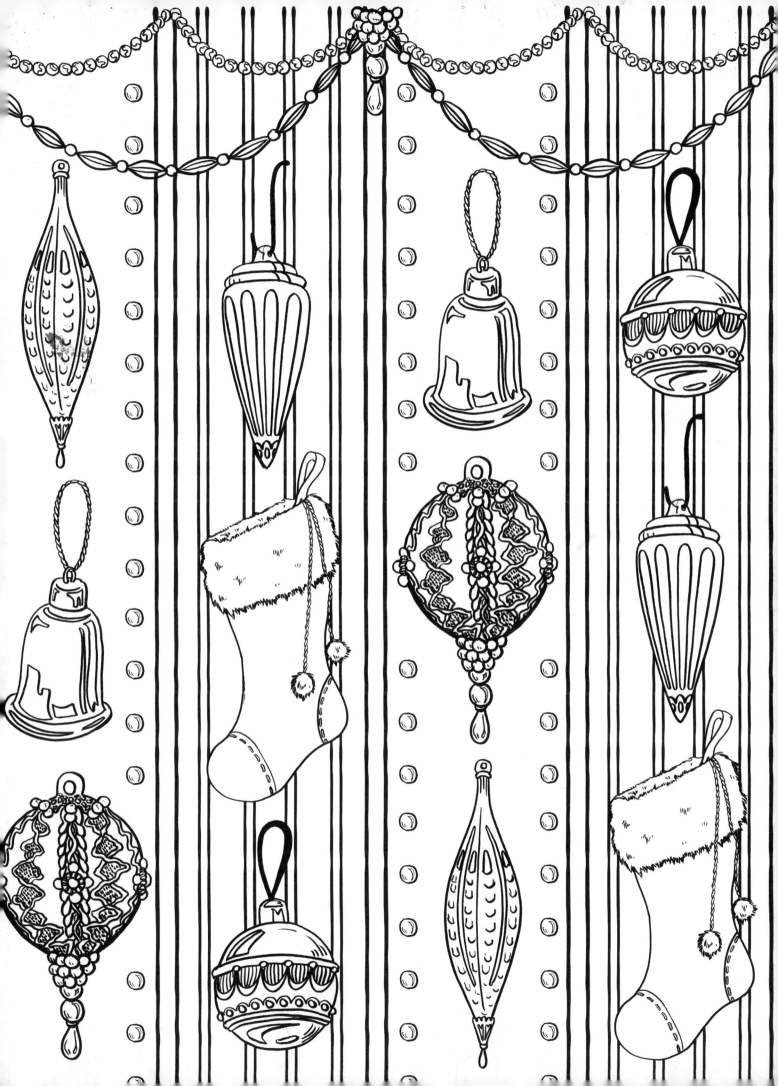

The table
under the tree
shone and flushed
with a thousand
different colours.

Fritz had been galloping round and round the room, trying his new bay horse.

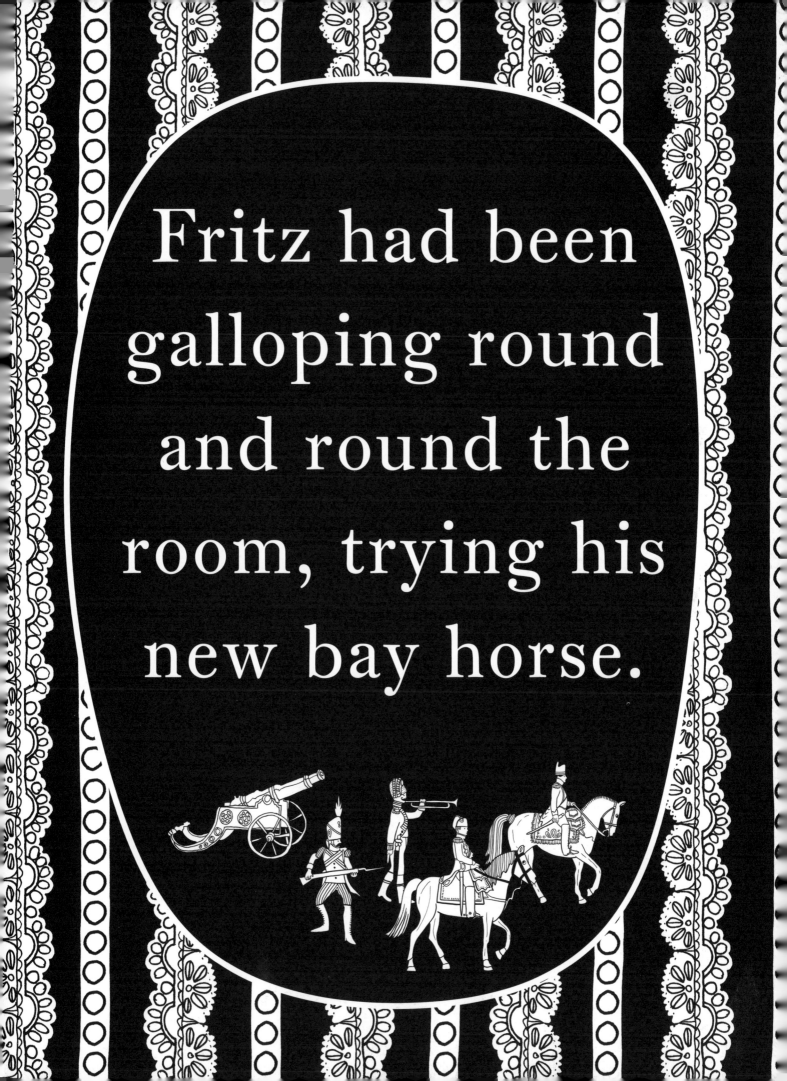

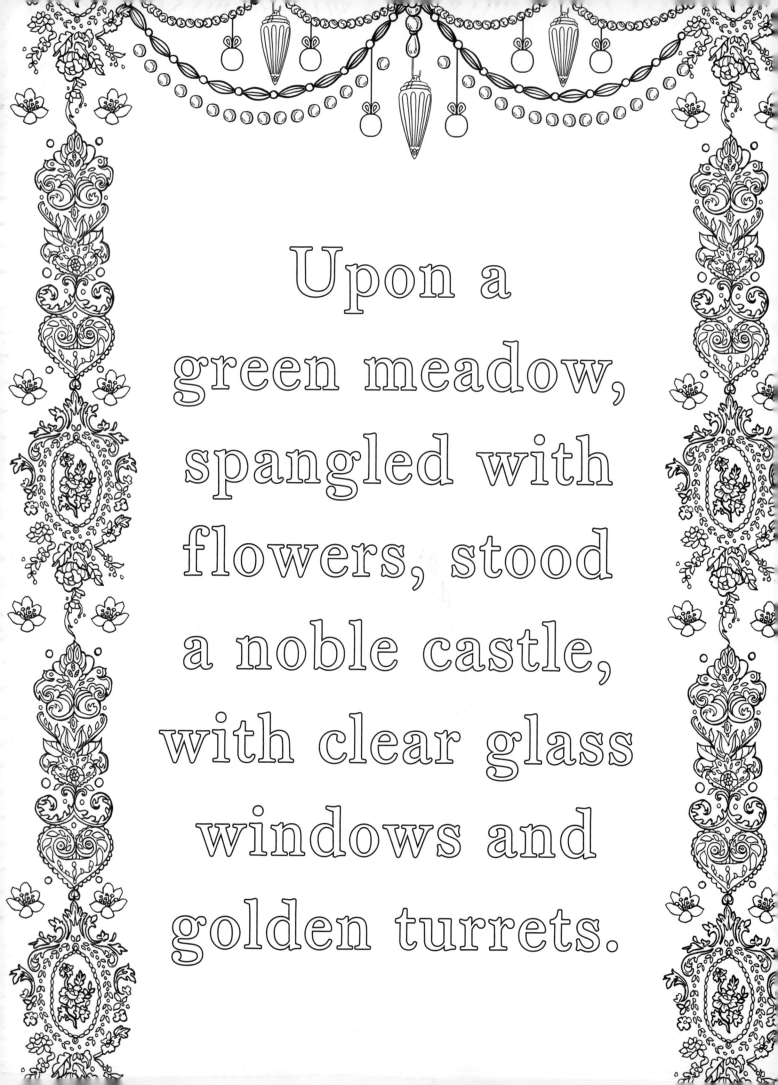

Upon a green meadow, spangled with flowers, stood a noble castle, with clear glass windows and golden turrets.

A curious
little man came into
view, who stood there
silent and retired,
as if he were waiting
quietly for his turn
to be noticed.

Clara
took him
immediately
in her arms.

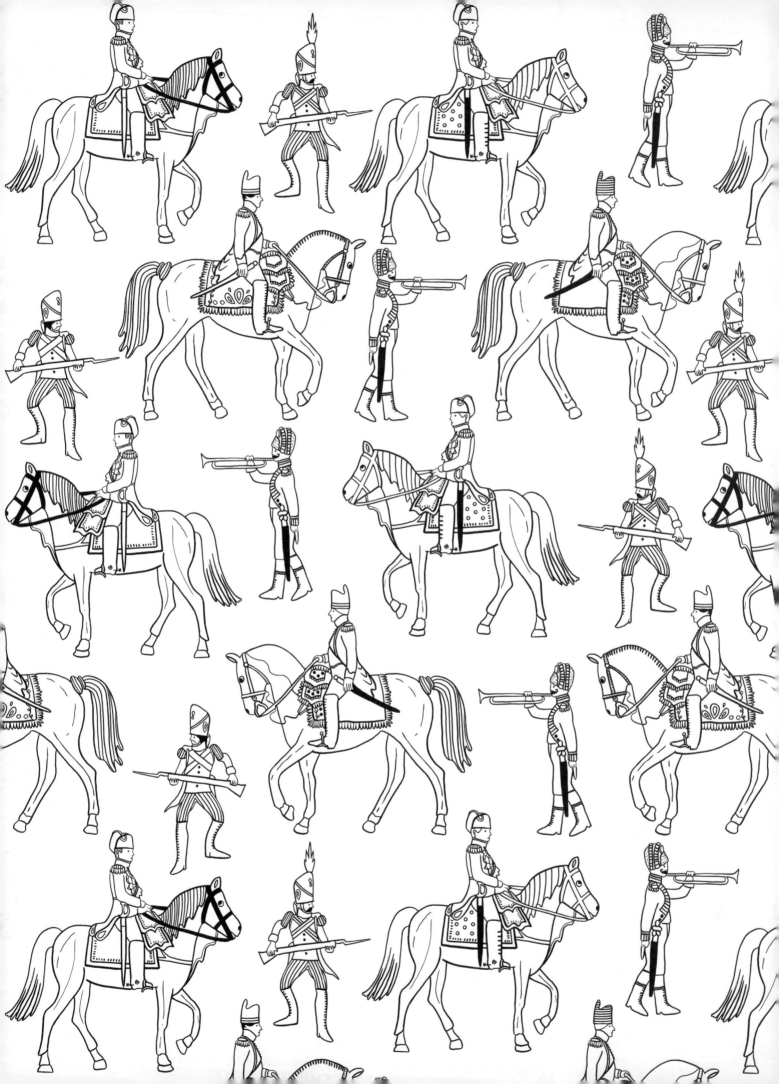

Seven mouse heads with seven crowns rose out from the floor.

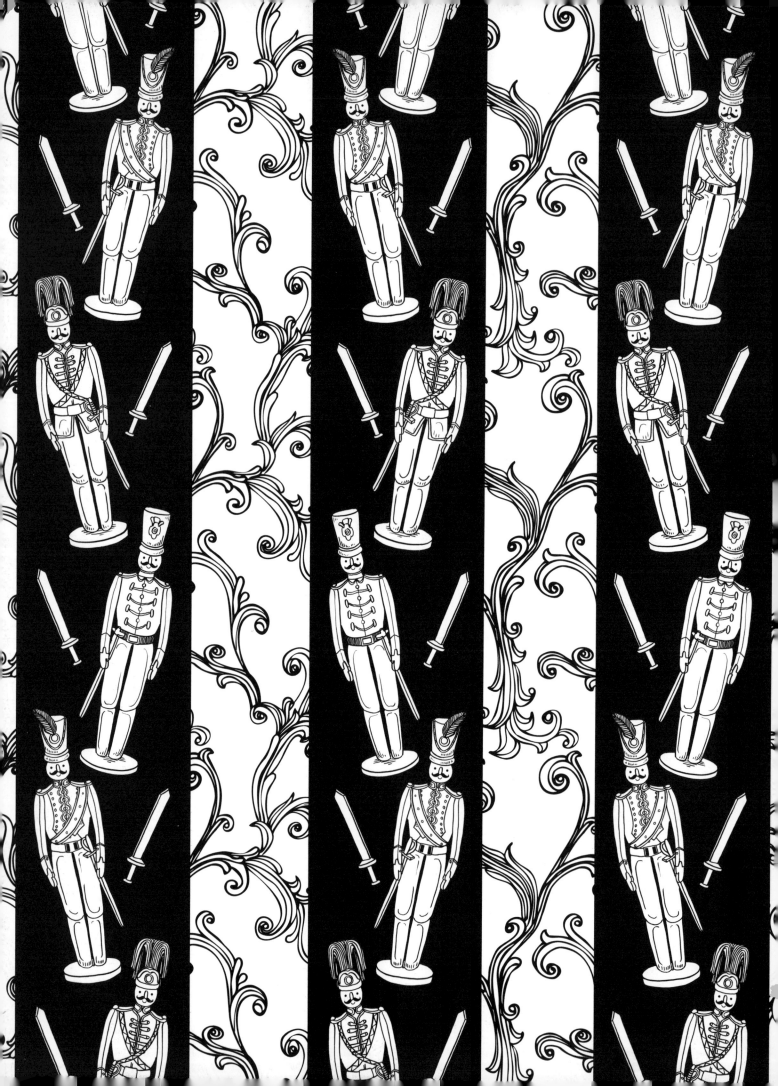

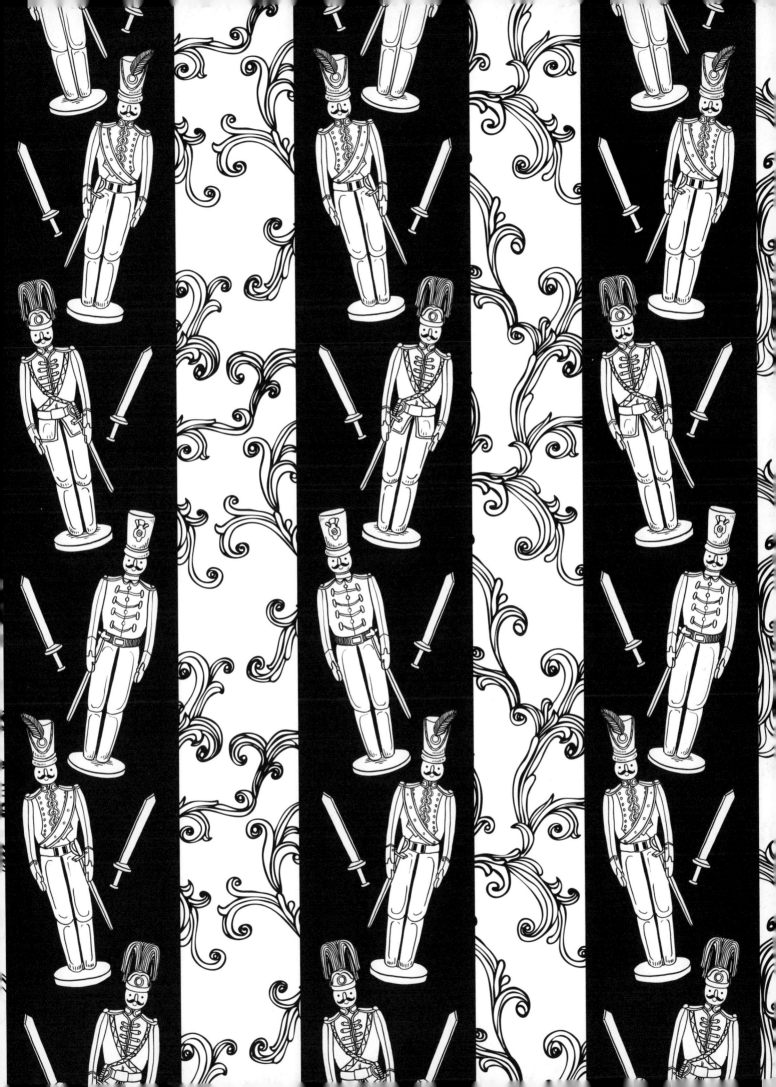

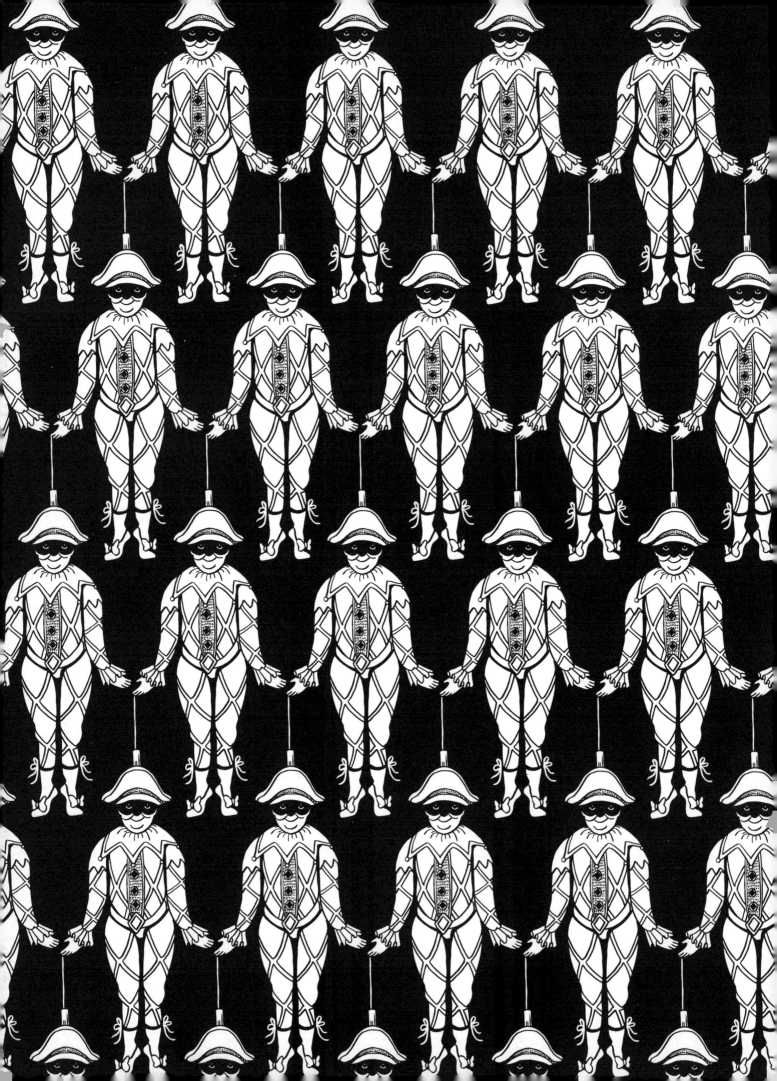

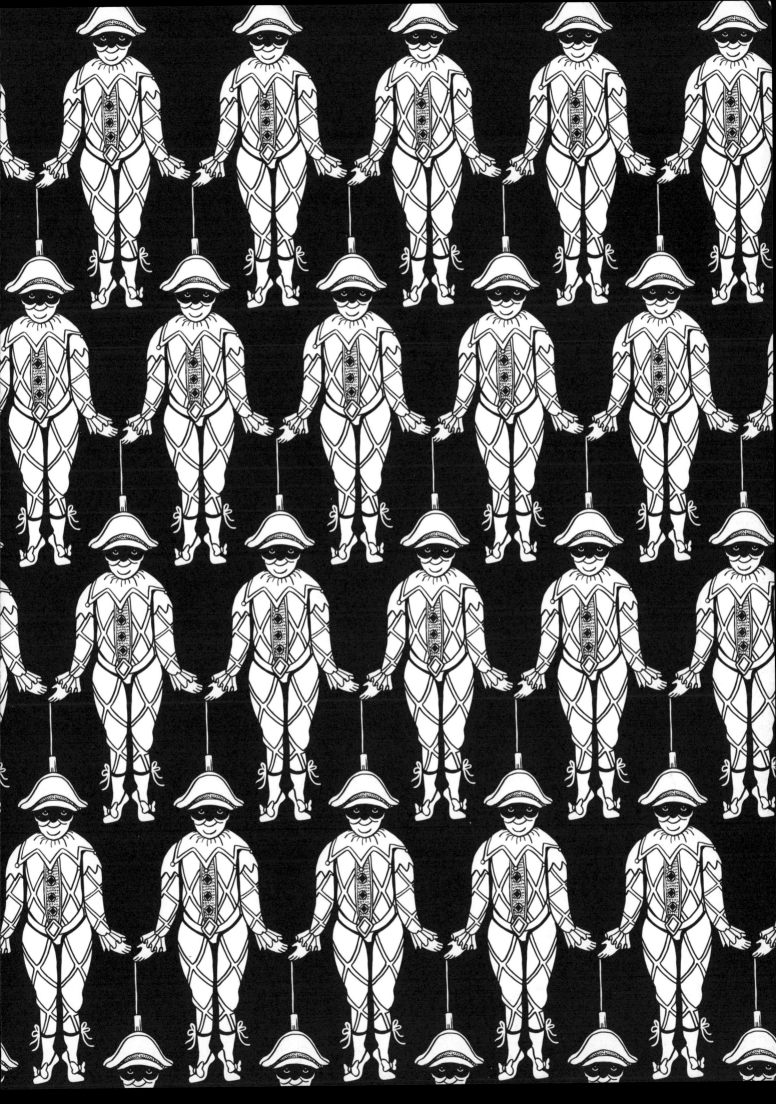

She stood upon a sweet-smelling meadow, surrounded by millions of sparks, which darted up like flashing jewels.

Beautiful silver-white swans with golden collars, swam over the lake singing sweet tunes.

They stood before a castle glimmering with rosy light, and crowned with a hundred airy towers.

The Nutcracker Prince showed Clara the land of sweets.

His
face was
as white
as milk,
and as red
as blood;
he wore a
handsome
red coat,
trimmed
with gold.

"You are a kind, good-natured young man; and, since you rule in such a charming land, among such pretty, merry people, I will be your bride."

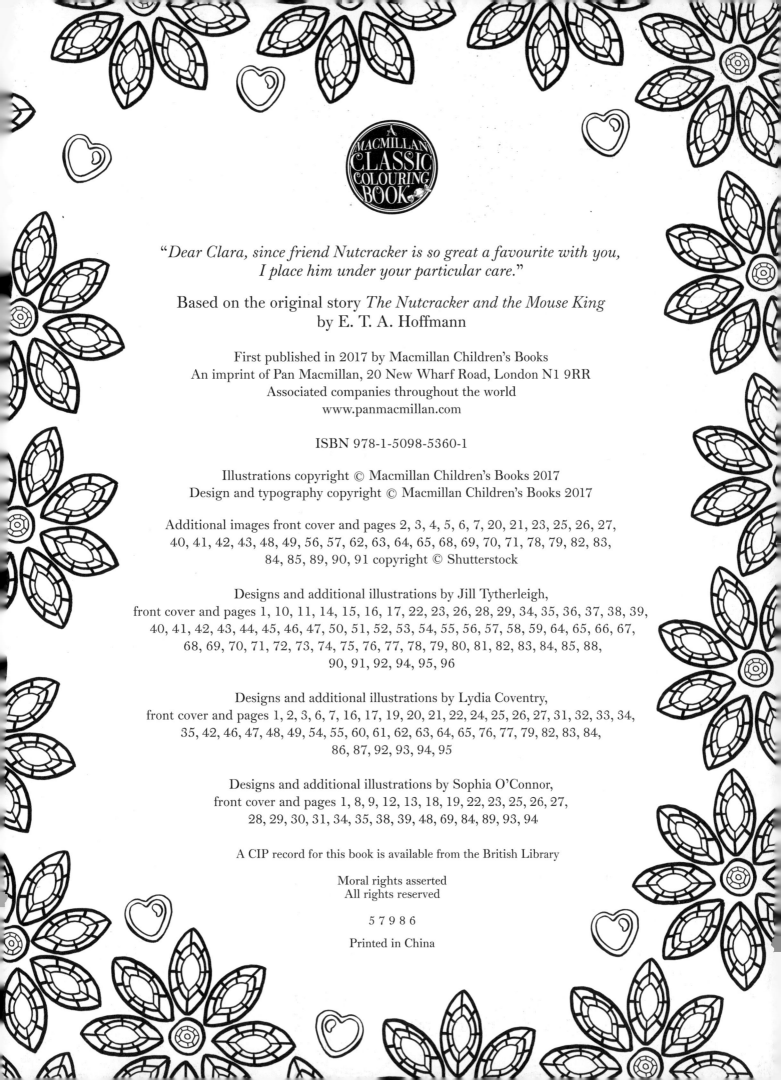

A
MACMILLAN
CLASSIC
COLOURING
BOOK

*"Dear Clara, since friend Nutcracker is so great a favourite with you,
I place him under your particular care."*

Based on the original story *The Nutcracker and the Mouse King*
by E. T. A. Hoffmann

First published in 2017 by Macmillan Children's Books
An imprint of Pan Macmillan, 20 New Wharf Road, London N1 9RR
Associated companies throughout the world
www.panmacmillan.com

ISBN 978-1-5098-5360-1

A CIP record for this book is available from the British Library

5 7 9 8 6

Printed in China

The story behind *The Nutcracker*

"It is nearly always the most improbable things that really come to pass."

E. T. A. HOFFMANN

Ernst Theodor Wilhelm Hoffmann was born in Königsberg, Prussia in 1776, the son of Christoph Ludwig Hoffmann, a barrister, and his wife Lovisa Albertina. Following his parents' separation in 1778 when Hoffmann was only two years old, he was brought up by his mother and his two aunts in the strict household of his uncle. He attended a Lutheran school where he showed great aptitude for classics, drawing, writing and piano-playing. In 1796, Hoffmann became a clerk for another of his uncles and worked first in Berlin and later in Poland. Here he married Marianna Tekla Michalina Rorer and they moved to Warsaw in 1804. Just two years later, Napoleon's troops captured Warsaw, and along with the other Prussian bureaucrats, Hoffmann lost his job and was forced to return to Berlin. Back in Germany, Hoffmann continued writing and composing and eventually had his breakthrough in 1810 when he was employed as a stagehand, decorator and playwright for the Bamberg Theatre. He began using the pseudonym E. T. A. Hoffmann, the 'A' standing for Amadeus in tribute to the composer Mozart whom he held in high regard. He spent a number of years working as a writer and composer before an argument cost him his job and he was forced to return to Berlin to pick up his previous career in law. His stories were heavily influenced by the tumultuous political landscape of his time and he was interested in exploring the darker side of humanity through his art. With recurring themes of the macabre and a blurring of the boundaries between fantasy and reality, Hoffmann's work presents a dark reflection of humanity. Hoffmann died in Berlin in 1822 at the age of 46.

"Dumas' version is famously more saccharine than Hoffmann's lugubrious tale" – Sarah Ardizzone, *Guardian*

ALEXANDRE DUMAS

Alexandre Dumas was born near Soissons, France in 1802. His father was a general in the French Revolutionary Army and died when Dumas was only four years old. He worked as a notary and then as a secretary to the Duke of Orléans who later became King Louis Philippe. During this time, he began writing plays, first in collaboration with Adolphe de Leuven, a poet and friend of Dumas, and later alone. He was strongly influenced by the works of Shakespeare and quickly became a successful playwright. Dumas was exiled from France for his involvement in the French Revolution of 1830 as the new king disapproved of his politics. Returning to Paris in the 1840s, he began writing fiction and produced some of his most renowned works during this time, including *The Three Musketeers* and *The Count of Monte Cristo*. Despite his wide success, Alexandre Dumas lived far beyond his means, especially in the latter years of his life. He remained in debt until his death in 1870. Dumas adapted Hoffmann's story *The Nutcracker and the Mouse King* in 1844, making the story lighter and more suitable for children. It is this adaptation that inspired *The Nutcracker* ballet and is the version of the story best known today.

"The Nutcracker's popularity lies principally in its surface enchantment, in the gorgeous nostalgia of its Christmas festivities and its fairytale transformations." – Judith Mackrell, *Guardian*

THE NUTCRACKER BALLET

The Nutcracker ballet was first performed at the Mayinsky Theatre in St. Petersburg, Russia in 1892 to a sell-out audience. Based on Alexandre Dumas's adaptation of E. T. A. Hoffmann's *The Nutcracker and the Mouse King*, the music was composed by world-famous Russian composer Pyotr Ilyich Tchaikovsky. Despite the big names behind the production, the ballet did not go down well with critics, many of whom claimed it was tedious and confusing. The ballet gained popularity when it was performed by the New York City Ballet in 1954, choreographed by George Balanchine, and it is now the most widely performed ballet in the world.